Magic ★ Toyshop

Special thanks to Sue Mongredien

First published in 2010 in *The Hoozles* series
First published in this edition in 2012
by Faber and Faber Ltd
Bloomsbury House
74–77 Great Russell Street
London WC1B 3DA

Printed and bound by CPI Group (UK) Ltd, Croydon, CR0 4YY
Series created by Working Partners Limited, London WC1X 9HH
Designed by Mandy Norman

A CIP record for this book
is available from the British Library

978–0–571–29459–6

FSC
www.fsc.org
MIX
Paper from
responsible sources
FSC® C101712

Magic Toyshop

My Magical Teddy

By Jessie Little

Illustrated by Penny Dann

ff

faber and faber

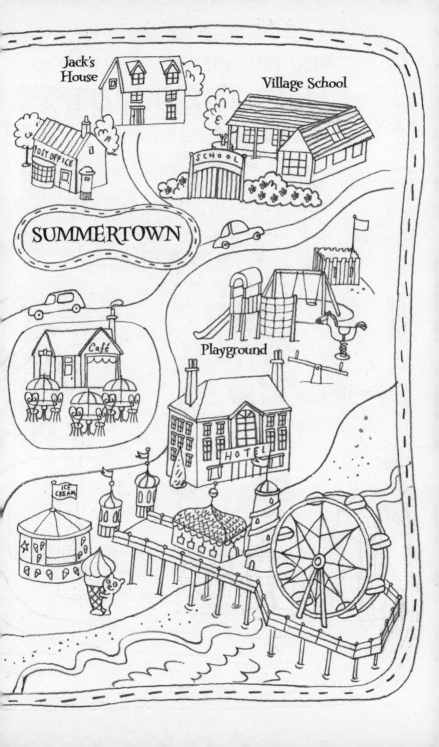

WHO LIVES IN SUMMERTOWN?
MEET THE HOOZLES!

This is
Willow and Toby

Here are Freddie
and Wobbly

Auntie Suzy
owns the toyshop!

The Hoozle Council – Grouchy, Wizard and Lovely

Nasty Croc is the
only mean Hoozle

Chapter One

'There she is! I can see her!' Seven-
year-old Willow Thompson waved
madly through the train window
as she caught a glimpse of her aunt
waiting on the platform. Auntie
Suzy's blonde curly hair looked

even wilder than usual, and she had on the biggest pair of sunglasses Willow had ever seen. 'Oh, I'm so excited!' she said, bouncing up and down as the train rumbled to a stop. 'A whole summer by the sea, with Auntie Suzy!'

Her mum smiled. 'You're going to have a wonderful time in Summertown,' she said, getting the bags down from the luggage rack.

'We are,' agreed Freddie, who was five. 'I can't wait to see Auntie Suzy's shop again and see if she's made any new Hoozles.'

Willow put on her backpack and hugged her mum goodbye. It was going to be strange, not spending the summer with her parents, but they had to travel abroad for a few months on business.

After her mum and dad, Auntie Suzy was Willow's favourite person. She was jolly and funny, made yummy chocolate biscuits, and had her very own toy shop on the ground floor of her house, filled with all sorts of brilliant toys. Willow thought it was the best toy shop in the world.

Auntie Suzy was there to meet them off the train, a big smile on her face. She wore a bright red dress, sparkly flip-flops and three different necklaces that glittered in the

sunshine.
'Hello
there!'
she cried,
flinging
her arms
around them. 'Oh,
what gorgeous long
hair you've got now,
Willow! And Freddie, aren't you
getting tall?'

'I've brought Wobbly,' Freddie said,
holding his cuddly lion up in the air.
Wobbly was a Hoozle – a special

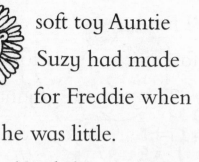

soft toy Auntie Suzy had made for Freddie when he was little.

'And I've got Toby,' Willow added, showing Auntie Suzy how her Hoozle was peeping out of her backpack. Toby was a blue teddy bear with a white nose and ears, and a little pocket on his front.

'Well, Willow, Freddie, Wobbly and Toby, it's good to see each and every one of you.' Auntie Suzy beamed.

'I just know this is going to be a fantastic summer for us all!'

They set off straight away for the sea-front, walking down a little hill from the train station. Willow smiled when she caught her first glimpse of the sunlight dancing on the waves. 'Look, Toby,' she said, turning to show him. 'There's the sea – and that's the beach where I found your pocket heart.'

Auntie Suzy smiled at Willow. 'That's right,' she said. 'And I've never seen such a pretty shell since then. It's as if you were meant to find it.'

Years ago, when Auntie Suzy had first made Toby, she'd told Willow that she needed to find something special to put in the pocket over his heart, to show how much they loved each other. Willow had found a white heart-shaped shell on the beach outside her aunt's shop and she'd known right away it was perfect for her Hoozle. The moment she put the glistening shell in Toby's pocket, Willow had felt very special,

tingly and warm and safe
all at once.

Seagulls swooped and screeched
overhead as they walked along the
sea-front. 'Nearly there,'
Auntie Suzy said. 'And I've
got a little surprise for you
two.'

Freddie blinked. 'A surprise?'

'Yes,' Auntie Suzy replied. 'Perfect
timing,' she went on, checking
her watch. 'Here we are. Good
afternoon, everybody!'

Willow was surprised to see a

crowd of people gathered outside
her aunt's shop – some of whom
let out a cheer as they saw Auntie
Suzy approaching. Then she noticed
that a few people in the crowd were
holding red sparkly balloons . . .
and that the old shop sign had been
covered up by red satin material,
with a ribbon dangling from one
end. What was going on?

Auntie Suzy bustled to the front
of the shop and took hold of the
ribbon. 'Willow, Freddie, come and
help,' she said. And then, with a

one-two-three, they pulled the
ribbon together and down fell
the red satin, revealing the shop's
new sign.

The Best Toy
Shop in the
World

OPEN

'The Best Toy Shop in the World,' Willow read aloud, then laughed. 'That's definitely the right name!' she declared with a grin.

Auntie Suzy gave her a squeeze. 'I think so too,' she said. 'Come on, everyone. Let's start the party!'

It is lovely to be back in Auntie Suzy's shop, Willow thought, as she and her brother went inside. Ricky, the friendly assistant, was

handing out paper cups
of lemonade and cookies to
celebrate the shop's re-opening,
and there was an excited buzz in
the air as everyone looked around.
There were wonderful rocking
horses with stitched leather saddles,
dolls' houses full of miniature
furniture, painted wooden castles
with knights and dragons. And, of
course, on a high shelf above the
counter sat Auntie Suzy's special
Hoozles, taking pride of place.

Willow always enjoyed seeing the Hoozles. She knew that each one was made for an individual customer, so there were only a few on display, but they'd been there for as long as she could remember and felt like old friends. One was white and grey and reminded Willow of an owl, with his wise yellow eyes. Another was a pink and purple pony Hoozle, with a lovely long mane. And there was a penguin-shaped Hoozle too, who was made from green and yellow velvet.

'Look, Toby,' Willow said, taking
him out of her backpack to show
him. She held Toby's soft round
paw and made him wave to his
Hoozle friends. But as she turned
back to the party, she saw a flash
of movement out of the corner of
her eye. A flicker, very fast, as if

something had moved up there on the shelf!

She straightened, Toby still in her hands, and stared up, her heart pounding. What was it that had moved? She was sure she'd seen something! It couldn't have been a Hoozle waving back, could it?

But the toys were quite still, their eyes gazing blankly down. After a few seconds, she looked away again, smiling at herself for making such a silly mistake. After all, everyone knew that soft toys couldn't move!

★ ★ ★

In bed that evening, Willow
snuggled under the patchwork quilt.
She was so happy to be back in the
attic room with its sloping ceiling
and the funny little window that
looked out over the beach.

She cuddled Toby and closed her
eyes, listening to the sound of the
sea outside.

'I'm glad you're
here with me,' she
murmured, her
fingers seeking out

the shell in his pocket and holding it for a moment.

Willow must have drifted off because the next thing she knew, she was rolling over in the darkness . . . and Toby wasn't there! She reached out sleepily – she always slept with him cuddled close – but couldn't find him. Then she heard a strange scuffling noise from somewhere down on the floor.

Willow flicked on her torch, aimed it towards the noise and nearly fell out of bed in surprise.

Toby was on the floor, but he wasn't lying on the carpet as she expected. He was up on his feet, and fighting with an orange crocodile toy!

He was actually moving, all by himself. Willow couldn't believe it.

'Get off me!' Toby growled, pushing the crocodile, who lurched backwards. 'And stay away from Willow!'

Willow sat up in shock. How could Toby talk?

'Toby?' Willow asked. 'What's going on?'

Toby turned towards her, and as he did so, Willow saw the crocodile shoot a sneaky arm out to tug at her bear's pocket heart.

'Toby! Watch out!' Willow cried.

Chapter Two

Toby knocked away the crocodile's hand just in time.

Willow reached for Toby, but the two toys were wrestling again and tumbled away.

'Leave my teddy bear alone!' Willow said, and as she got out of bed, the crocodile growled and then skidded out of the room.

Willow ran to Toby, scooping him up in her arms. Usually he was soft and cuddly but now he was stiff with anger, his fur standing on end.

'Toby, I can't believe it. You're alive!' Willow said. This was the most amazing thing that had ever happened to her.

Toby was glaring over his shoulder at where the crocodile had run away. 'That orange bully doesn't frighten me!'

Willow stroked his fur. 'I don't understand,' she admitted. 'You can talk . . . and move! How?'

Toby relaxed and nuzzled against her hand. 'Yes,' he said simply. 'And you can hear me. I knew you were special, Willow.'

'Oh, Toby!' Willow cried, hugging him. She had always talked to Toby as if he could hear her — and now it turned out he'd been able to all along! 'But why was that orange crocodile trying to grab your shell?'

'I don't know,' Toby said. He glared again for a moment, and

 Willow couldn't help but think how adorable he looked when he

was cross. 'But don't worry about him, Willow. I won't let him near you again.'

'We'll have to make sure he can't get in again,' Willow said. She made sure the door was shut tight before switching off the torch and cuddling up in bed.

'Goodnight, Toby,' she murmured.

'Goodnight, Willow,' Toby replied. 'I love you.'

'I love you too, Toby.'

But it took Willow a long while to fall asleep again. Thoughts were rushing through her head. Where had that orange crocodile come from? And why did it want Toby's pocket heart?

★ ★ ★

'Willow! Willow! Are you awake?'

Willow stirred. 'Toby?' she murmured, opening her eyes. But the voice came from Freddie, who was standing by her bed, clutching his Hoozle and looking unhappy.

'Are you all right?' Willow asked, rubbing the sleep from her eyes. 'What's up?'

'I want to go home,' he said. 'Wobbly's broken – he's gone all cold. He doesn't feel right any more.'

Wobbly looked the same as ever to Willow but she didn't say so, as Freddie seemed really upset. She swung her legs out of bed. 'Maybe if you cuddle him, he'll warm up?' she suggested.

But Freddie shook his head. 'Come on, let's have some breakfast. Remember Auntie Suzy's bacon sandwiches? I bet you won't want to go home after one of those.'

She picked up Toby, then took Freddie's hand and led him downstairs. They could hear Auntie Suzy singing along to the radio in the kitchen and sure enough, there was a delicious smell of bacon wafting through the house.

Auntie Suzy was wearing a big red dressing gown and buttering

some toast. 'Morning, you two!' she cried. 'Breakfast's almost ready.'

Freddie sat down at the kitchen table, but Willow went and spoke to her aunt in a low voice. 'Freddie's feeling a bit sad this morning. Could he borrow a toy from the shop to play with? I can pop down and get one, if that's okay.'

'Of course,' Auntie Suzy said. 'The door's always open, Willow.'

Willow ran down to the shop. When she'd shut the door behind

her, Toby suddenly spoke. 'I know what's wrong with Wobbly,' he said.

Willow jumped at his voice. Since seeing Freddie's sad little face, she'd almost forgotten her Hoozle was alive. 'His pocket heart has been stolen; I can tell. That sneaky orange crocodile must have taken it!'

The events of the night before rushed into Willow's mind and she felt tingly with excitement all over again. But then Toby's words about the crocodile sank in, and she realised what bad news this was.

'Oh, no!' she said. 'We've got to get it back. But how?'

There was a small cough from above their heads, and Willow looked up to see the grey and white Hoozle peering down at her with his wise-looking eyes. 'Perhaps we can help?' he said.

Chapter Three

Willow almost fell over in shock.
'You . . . you can talk as well!' she
gasped, staring up at the top shelf.

The grey and white Hoozle
smiled broadly, his eyes crinkling
at the corners. 'And you can hear,'
he said, as Toby had done the night

before. 'It's wonderful. I haven't known a human who could talk to us since Suzy.'

Toby winked. 'I said you were special, Willow.'

Willow blinked as she noticed the other two Hoozles were whispering and nudging each other, too. They were all alive! 'Is this really happening?' she managed to get out. 'It's not just a dream?'

The old grey and white Hoozle chuckled. 'It's not a dream,' he assured her. 'Allow me to introduce myself. I'm called Wizard, and I'm the first Hoozle Suzy ever made. I'm head of the Hoozle Council,' he added, puffing his round chest out with pride.

'Nice to meet you, Wizard,' Willow said, still feeling dazed.

'And I'm called Lovely,' the pink pony-shaped Hoozle said, tossing her purple mane and batting her long eyelashes. 'Your mum and I spent many happy wonderful days together when she was a little girl. You remind me of her, you know. You're just as pretty!'

'I'm Grouchy,' the penguin Hoozle said, with a little flap of his green velvety wings. 'It's a long time since we've had a human to talk to.'

Willow realised that she was
staring with her mouth wide open,
and closed it with a snap. 'H-hi,'
she said after a moment. 'Wow!' An
excited thrill was whirling up inside
her. 'Can all Hoozles talk?'

Wizard nodded. 'Oh
yes,' he replied.
'Suzy has made
lots of
Hoozles for
customers
over

the years. They live all over Summertown.' He turned to Lovely and Grouchy. 'Let's climb down. I think we need a proper chat with Willow.'

Willow watched in delight as the three Hoozles clambered down from the shelf and on to the counter. Wizard and Grouchy climbed slowly and carefully but Lovely took flying leaps from shelf to shelf, her mane swinging behind her as she jumped. 'Wheee!' she cried, landing on the lap of a plush teddy bear, then

galloping across the roof of a dolls'
house. 'Oh, it feels so good to run!'

'We can't stay for long. Willow's
got to have breakfast soon,' Toby
put in. 'But something awful has
happened. Last night, an orange
crocodile Hoozle tried to steal my
pocket heart. I fought him off, but
Wobbly wasn't so lucky. What can
we do?'

Grouchy put a velvet wing over
his own pocket heart at the news,
looking horrified. 'Must have been
that terrible Croc,' he said, shuffling

over to join the other Hoozles.

Wizard nodded. 'Croc – the crocodile you saw – is a very sad case,' he explained. 'He was abandoned by his owner and has turned against his fellow Hoozles.

I've long suspected that he's on a mission to steal the pocket hearts of all the Hoozles in the town and is hiding them in secret places.'

'He must have heard about Toby and Wobbly coming to town,' Grouchy put in. 'Thought he'd try and get two more pocket hearts.' He clicked his beak with a grumpy little snap. 'The cheek!'

'But why is he after the pocket hearts?' Willow asked.

Toby scratched his ear with his big blue paw. 'My pocket heart

is a symbol of the
friendship between
you and me. And
without it . . .' He
gave a shiver. 'It
would be like losing
our friendship. I

would feel so sad – like all the
specialness had gone and I was all
alone.'

'Poor Wobbly,' Lovely said,
shaking her long tail.

'And poor Freddie,' Willow said,
remembering how unhappy her

brother had been. 'No wonder he's so sad.' She squared her shoulders. 'Well, I'll find Wobbly's pocket heart. It's a little white football; I'd know it anywhere. Where does Croc live? I'll ask Auntie Suzy to take us there this morning!'

There was a small silence. Lovely trotted over to Willow and rubbed her soft head against her. 'You are kind,' she said. 'But we don't know where Croc lives. And . . . well, the little football could be anywhere. But ask Wobbly. Hoozles have a strong connection to their pocket hearts. He might be able to give you a clue.'

'Willow! Breakfast's on the table!' came Auntie Suzy's voice just then.

Willow grabbed a robot toy she thought Freddie would like, then picked up Toby. 'I'd better go,' she told the others. 'We've got some important work to do this morning, Toby. We're going to find Wobbly's pocket heart and put it back where it belongs – we've just got to!'

Chapter Four

Upstairs in the warm, sunny
kitchen, Willow found her aunt and
brother eating bacon sandwiches.
Willow set the robot down in front
of her brother and picked up his
lion-shaped Hoozle for a closer
look. 'Poor old Wobbly,' she said,

trying to sound casual. 'What's
wrong with you, then?' She peeped
into his pocket, and sure enough,
the little white football was missing.
'His pocket heart has gone,' she said
to Freddie. 'That's why he doesn't
feel right.'

'But I didn't take it out,' Freddie said.

'Do you know where it is, Wobbly?' Willow asked the lion Hoozle. She held Wobbly up to her ear, hoping he'd whisper the answer but he didn't say anything.

'It's okay,' Toby whispered to Wobbly, from where he was in her other hand. 'You can tell her – she understands. She's special.'

Willow felt Wobbly tense slightly in her arms. He had definitely heard that! Her heart thumped and then

. . . 'It's guarded by the lion,' came
the reply, in a tiny whisper of a roar.

She kissed his soft yellow head . . .
then realised that both Freddie and
Auntie Suzy were looking at her
strangely.

'Willow,' Freddie scoffed, as if she'd
gone mad. 'Toys don't talk!'

Willow hesitated, and noticed that
Auntie Suzy was looking straight at
her, her eyebrows raised.

'Oh I don't know,' Auntie Suzy
said, her eyes sparkling. 'Maybe if we
love our toys lots and lots, they can.'

Willow remembered what the
other Hoozles had told her about
Suzy.

'And Hoozles are very special
toys,' Willow replied.

A delighted smile spread across

her aunt's face. 'Perhaps Willow's playing a game,' Auntie Suzy suggested. 'What did Wobbly say, Willow?'

'That the football's being guarded by a lion,' Willow replied.

'Did he now?' Auntie Suzy said. Willow realised that her aunt might know exactly what had happened.

'It must be at the zoo!' Freddie said.

Auntie Suzy shook her head. 'There isn't a zoo for miles around here.'

'Are there any
lions nearby?'
Willow asked.

Auntie Suzy thought
for a moment. 'There are
lots of animals in the park down
the road,' she said. 'Not real ones –
animal rides in the playground. I'm
not sure if there's a lion there or not.'
She caught Willow's eye and smiled.
'We'll go there this morning and
find out.'

★ ★ ★

After breakfast, they set off for the
playground. There were swings and
slides and a sandpit and . . . Willow's
heart thumped as she spotted a
safari carousel, where you could sit
on big plastic animals. 'Look, Toby,'
she whispered. 'Cross your paws
there's a lion on it!' She saw Toby
wink and cross his arms over his
chest.

Willow felt shivery with
excitement as she saw the sandy-
coloured lion with its rippling plastic
mane, and majestic expression.
'Right,' she murmured to Toby,
getting him out of her backpack.
'Now to find Wobbly's pocket heart.'

'Hello, Suzy,' called a friendly
man who was in charge of the ride.
'Do your young friends want a go?'

'Yes, please,' Willow said.

While the man helped Freddie
on to the ride, Willow checked all
over the plastic lion for the football,

even propping Toby underneath it
so that he could peer into the areas
she couldn't. But she couldn't spot a
single place where Croc might have
hidden the tiny ball. The big lion
was shiny and smooth without any
holes or crevices that would make

a good hiding place. 'Any luck?' she
murmured to Toby.

'No,' he growled quietly in reply.

Freddie had clambered on to the
elephant seat by now, and Auntie
Suzy was paying for them to have
a ride, so Willow climbed on to the

lion, thinking hard. She sat Toby
on her lap so that they could talk
quietly while the carousel went
round.

'This must be the wrong lion,' she murmured to her Hoozle. 'But where else might a lion be?'

'I'm not sure,' Toby said, scratching his ear. 'But it's not a big town. The ball can't be far from the shop, can it?'

'No,' said Willow, racking her brain for ideas. But none came – and before she knew it, the carousel ride was over and it was time to get off.

Auntie Suzy held Freddie's hands as he jumped down. 'Feeling better now, Freddie?' she asked.

He gave a small smile. 'A bit,' he said. 'But Wobbly doesn't.'

'Well, we'll have to look somewhere else for the lion,' Suzy said. 'Let's do it while I do a bit of shopping.'

They left the park and headed along the high street.

All of a sudden, Willow saw something that made her heart skip a beat . . . a stone lion outside the town hall, at the top of a wide flight of steps! Toby gave a quiet

little cheer from her backpack, and
Willow grinned. Another lion. Was
this one guarding Wobbly's pocket
heart?

Chapter Five

'Auntie Suzy?' Willow asked. 'Could I go and see that stone lion up there?'

Auntie Suzy smiled. 'Okay,' she replied. 'Freddie and I will be at the grocer's — it's just around the corner, see?'

Willow nodded. 'I'll be really quick,' she promised and ran up the stone steps two at a time. Once again, she felt herself tingle with anticipation. 'Right, Toby,' she said, unzipping him from her backpack. 'Eyes peeled!'

She reached the lion and stretched up to prop Toby on its back. 'See if the football is anywhere in his mane,' she whispered, while she began searching all around the lion's base. Perhaps the football was balanced on his big stone paws?

Tucked in with his thick stone tail?
But neither guess was right.

'Anything?' she hissed to Toby.

'Not a sausage,' he replied and
rolled off, landing in Willow's hands.

Willow sighed in frustration
and ran back down to find Auntie
Suzy and Freddie. 'Croc has found
a really good hiding place,' she
groaned. 'I'm starting to think
we're never going to be able to fix
Wobbly!'

After the grocer's, they set off
home. Willow was deep in thought,

unable to stop thinking about Wobbly's pocket heart. Did Wobbly get it wrong about the lion? she wondered. Or had she misheard him? Maybe he'd said 'line', not 'lion' or . . .

'Oh!' Freddie exclaimed suddenly, jerking Willow out of her thoughts. 'Wobbly is feeling warmer now.'

'That's good news,' Auntie Suzy said, with a sidelong glance at Willow.

Willow wasn't sure why her aunt had such a twinkle in her eye, but

Toby explained in a whisper, 'I think
Wobbly's feeling warmer because
we're getting close to his pocket
heart.'

Willow gazed around eagerly at
once, back on the lion-hunt. Freddie
had stopped in front of a pet shop

window and was pointing out some lizards to Auntie Suzy, but Willow felt too impatient to look. There wouldn't be a lion in the pet shop!

In the very next moment, Willow stopped short. Not far from the pet shop was a smart town house, and on its front door was a shiny brass knocker in the shape of a lion's head.

With shaking hands, Willow got Toby out of her backpack and held him in front of her so that he could see too. She checked that nobody was watching and edged closer to the house. There were two steps leading up to the door . . . no, the little football wasn't balanced on either of them. There was a big brass letterbox — surely Croc hadn't popped the pocket heart through there? They'd never find it if he had.

Where else might he have hidden the ball?

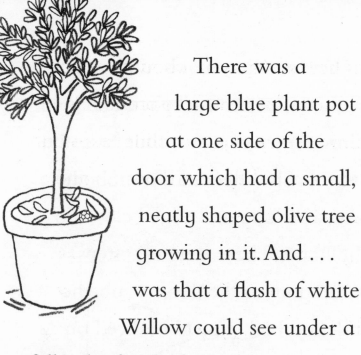

There was a
large blue plant pot
at one side of the
door which had a small,
neatly shaped olive tree
growing in it. And . . .
was that a flash of white
Willow could see under a
fallen leaf near the trunk?

She crouched down and picked up
the leaf, her fingers shaking. There,
underneath, was the little football.

'Oh, yes!' she cried in excitement
and reached out to get it. But just

as her fingers were about to touch
it, there was a flash of orange as
Croc the orange crocodile leapt out
from behind the plant pot . . . and
snatched it away!

Chapter Six

'Oh no you don't!' the orange
Hoozle snarled, clutching the
football between his paws.

Willow gasped. 'Croc! Give that
back at once!'

Croc sneered. 'Ahh, you can hear
me, can you?' he said. 'Well, listen

to this: I'm going to get your bear's pocket heart next. You just see if I don't!'

Willow held Toby protectively. His fur was standing on end with rage. 'You'll never get Toby's pocket heart,' she told Croc.

'And why would you want to?'
Toby asked, eyes blazing. 'Why
would you do such a terrible thing?'

Croc gave a scornful laugh. 'It's
for your own good,' he told Toby.
'Children are horrible creatures
who can't be trusted to look after
Hoozles. Without your pocket heart,
she won't love you so much – and
you'll survive!'

'What do you mean, he'll survive?'
Willow asked indignantly. 'I love
Toby – I'd never do anything to
harm him.'

'Ha,' Croc snorted. 'That's the problem. Children love us Hoozles so much, they love us to bits! All that cuddling . . . our fur gets worn, our stitches are torn, our eyes fall off . . .'

'I love it when Willow cuddles me,' Toby replied. 'I don't care what it does to my fur.'

'Well, I think love is stupid,' Croc snapped. 'I hope no one ever tries to love me.'

He was about to run off when Willow grabbed him and picked him up. 'Get off!' Croc yelped, squirming in her grasp and trying to prise her fingers off him . . . but as he did so, he let go of the football which bounced away down the pavement.

Willow put Croc down immediately and ran to chase after the ball. It rolled into the

gutter, then came to a stop against
a car tyre. Willow snatched it up.
Yes! She'd got Wobbly's pocket
heart back! She caught sight of

Croc slinking behind the plant
pot looking furious, and stuck her

tongue out at him, before rushing to her brother. 'Freddie, look what I've found!' she cried.

Freddie was still peering into the pet shop, but his face lit up when he saw what was in Willow's hand. 'Wobbly's pocket heart!' he shouted excitedly. He put it into Wobbly's pocket and Willow was sure she saw

a little smile on the lion Hoozle's face. Then Freddie hugged Willow. 'Thank you,' he said. 'Wobbly feels much better now!'

Auntie Suzy beamed at Willow, and came over to hug her too. 'I'm very proud of you,' she said quietly, dropping a kiss on to Willow's head.

Willow snuggled into her aunt, feeling very happy. What an adventure!

'I knew you could do it, Willow,' Toby murmured, resting his soft head against her arm. 'Well done you!'

A few minutes later, they were

back at the toy shop. When Willow walked in, she went straight over to where Wizard, Lovely and Grouchy were sitting back on their shelf and made a secret thumbs-up sign to them. 'I did it,' she whispered.

Wizard gave Willow a tiny wink and she thought she might burst with pride. How she loved being friends with the Hoozles!

The shop bell jingled just then as a customer came in, and Willow turned to see a boy about the same age as her, with his mum.

They browsed through the toys for a while, then the boy noticed the Hoozles up on the shelf . . . and a smile broke over his face. 'Mum, come and look at these,' he said.

His mum gazed up at the Hoozles. 'Aren't they lovely?' she said. 'They look so cuddly.'

'They're called Hoozles,' Auntie Suzy said, overhearing. 'And they're all different. If you're interested, I could make you your very own Hoozle.'

'Would you like one as a moving-in present, Jack?' the boy's mum asked, ruffling the boy's hair.

Jack nodded shyly. 'Yes, please,' he said.

Willow smiled. A new Hoozle? She would do her best to protect that one then, as well as Toby, and all the other Hoozles in the town.

She smiled to herself and stroked
Toby's soft fur as she held him close.
It was going to be a busy summer,
all right – but if today was anything
to go by, Willow was quite sure
it was also going to be the most
exciting summer of her whole life!

Magic Toyshop

Get ready for even more

Magic Toyshop adventures!

Magic
Toyshop
Ragbag Friends

Jessie Little

Magic
Toyshop
The Rabbit Rescue

Jessie Little

Magic
Toyshop
Treasure Island Trouble

Jessie Little